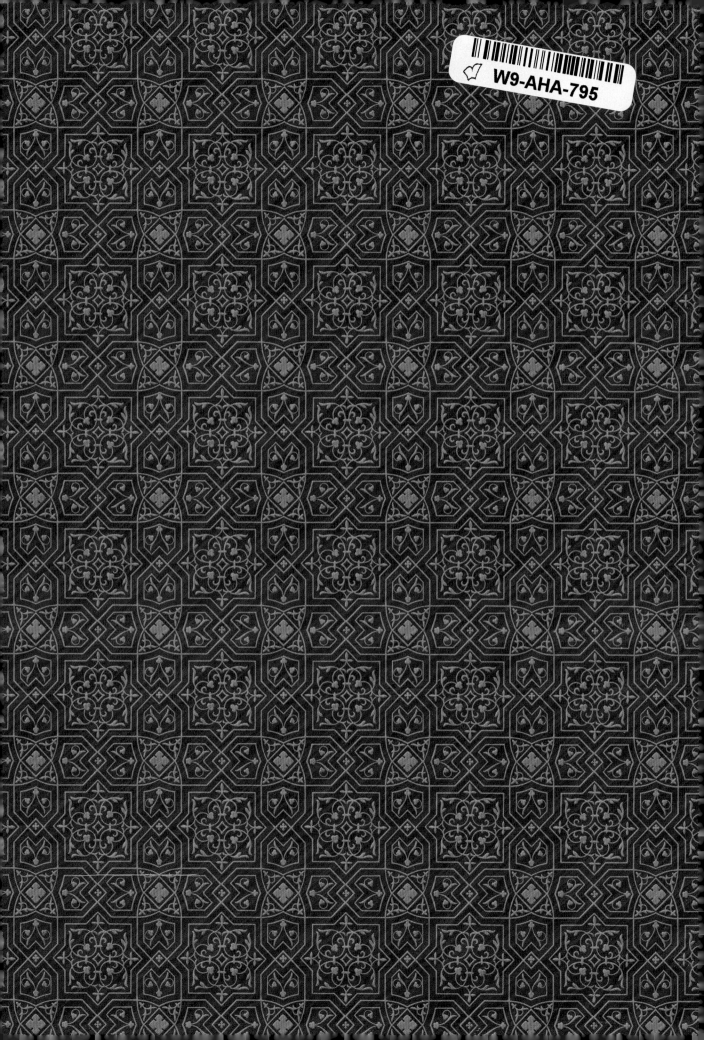

Harry Potter™

HOGWARTS
AND BEYOND
POSTER BOOK

SCHOLASTIC INC.
New York   Toronto   London   Auckland   Sydney
Mexico City   New Delhi   Hong Kong   Buenos Aires

ISBN-13: 978-0-545-08218-1 ISBN-10: 0-545-08218-8

12 11 10 9 8 7 6 5 4 3 2 1   9 10 11/0

Art Direction by Rick DeMonico
Book Design by Heather Barber

Printed in Singapore First printing, June 2009

Contents

PART I
LIFE AT HOGWARTS™

STUDENT PORTRAITS

Harry Potter™

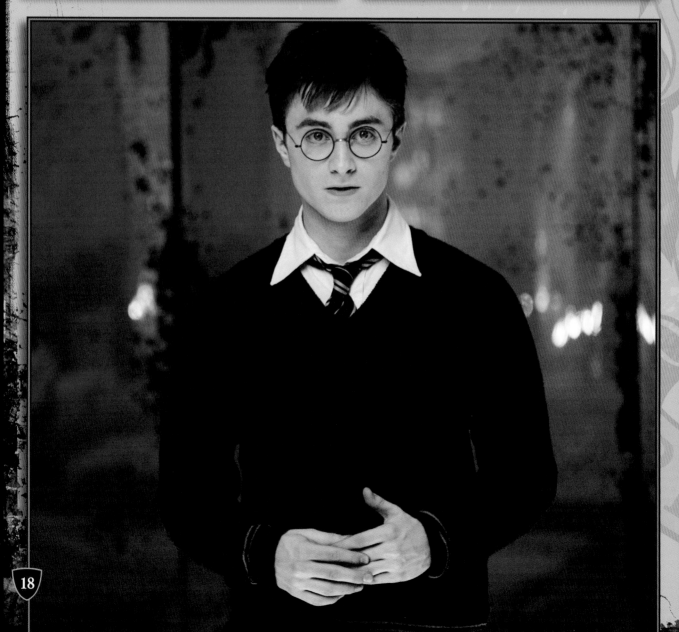

Hermione Granger™

GRYFFI

Ron Weasley™

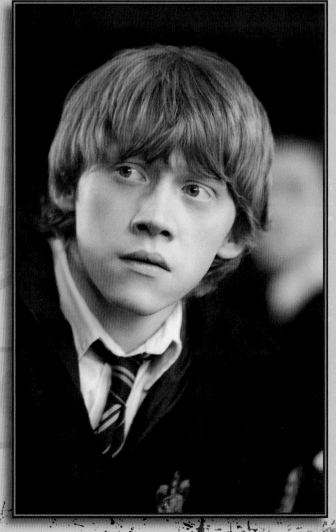

Ginny Weasley™

Fred & George Weasley

Neville Longbottom™

Seamus Finnigan

Dean Thomas

Romilda Vane

Cormac McLaggen

Lavender Brown™

Padma Patil

Parvati Patil

Draco Malfoy™

Vincent Crabbe

Gregory Goyle

Blaise Zabini

Cedric Diggory

Marcus Belby

Cho Chang

Luna Lovegood™

RAVENCLAW

HOGWARTS™
CASTLE
AND GROUNDS

Hogwarts Castle

The Fat Lady

Library

The Great Hall

The Chamber of Secrets™

Gryffindor™ common room

Corridors and staircases

49

Quidditch™ pitch

Potions classroom

Hospital wing

Room of Requirement

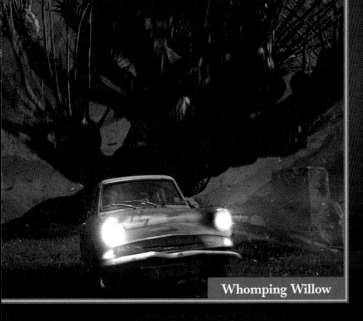

Whomping Willow

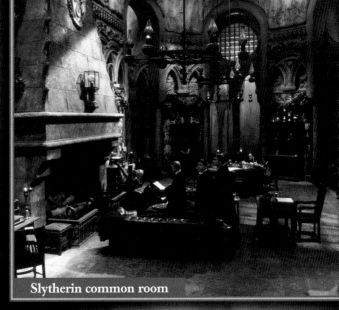

Slytherin common room

Owlery

Hagrid's hut

Forbidden Forest

STAFF AT HOGWARTS™

ALBUS DUMBLEDORE™
Headmaster

MINERVA McGONAGALL™
Deputy Headmistress, Transfiguration teacher,
Head of Gryffindor house

RUBEUS HAGRID™
Keeper of Keys and Grounds and
Care of Magical Creatures teacher

SEVERUS SNAPE™
Defense Against the Dark Arts teacher and
Head of Slytherin house

FILIUS FLITWICK
Charms teacher and
Head of Ravenclaw house

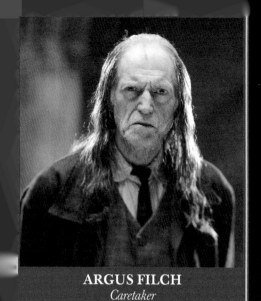

ARGUS FILCH
Caretaker

MADAM POMFREY
Hospital wing matron

SIBYLL TRELAWNEY
Divination teacher

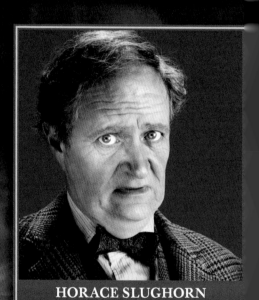

HORACE SLUGHORN
Potions master

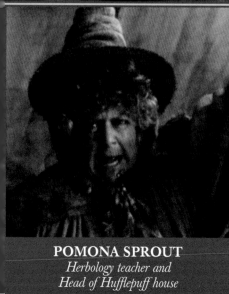

POMONA SPROUT
*Herbology teacher and
Head of Hufflepuff house*

MADAM HOOCH
Flying teacher and Quidditch referee

Defense Against the Dark Arts Teachers:

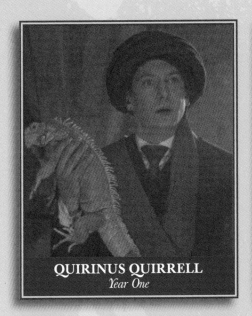

QUIRINUS QUIRRELL
Year One

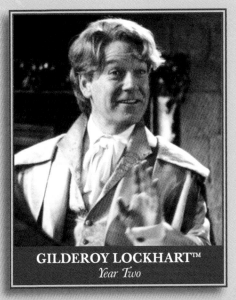

GILDEROY LOCKHART™
Year Two

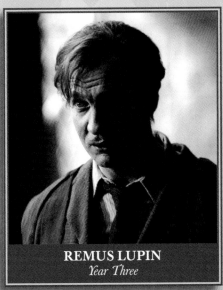

REMUS LUPIN
Year Three

ALASTOR "MAD-EYE" MOODY
Year Four

DOLORES UMBRIDGE™
Year Five

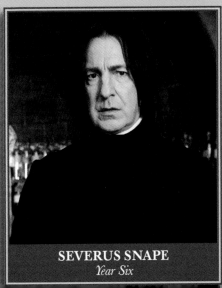

SEVERUS SNAPE
Year Six

STUDENT LIFE

Dumbledore's Army

Quidditch

The Slug Club™

The Yule Ball

THROUGH THE YEARS

Year One

Year Two

Year Three

Year Four

Year Five

Year Six

PART II

THE WIZARDING WORLD

THE ORDER OF THE PHOENIX™

Albus Dumbledore, Head of the Order of the Phoenix

Severus Snape

Remus Lupin

Kingsley Shacklebolt

Arthur Weasley

Molly Weasley

Sirius Black™

Nymphadora Tonks™

Alastor "Mad-Eye" Moody

Minerva McGonagall

VOLDEMORT™
& THE
DEATH EATERS

Lord Voldemort

Lucius Malfoy

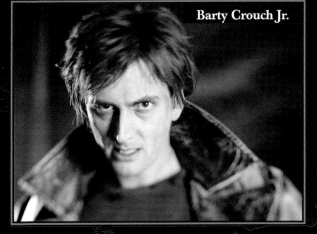

Barty Crouch Jr.

Peter Pettigrew

Bellatrix Lestrange

Fighting Dark Forces

Harry battles the Basilisk
in the Chamber of Secrets.

Harry destroys Tom Riddle's diary.

Harry fights a Boggart in the form of a Dementor.

Harry conjures a Patronus.

Ron is held captive by a Death Eater in the Ministry of Magic's Department of Mysteries.

The Death Eaters wreak havoc at the Quidditch World Cup.

Harry and his friends fight Death Eaters in the Ministry of Magic's Hall of Prophecy.

Harry is possessed by Lord Voldemort.

Lord Voldemort conjures a fireball.

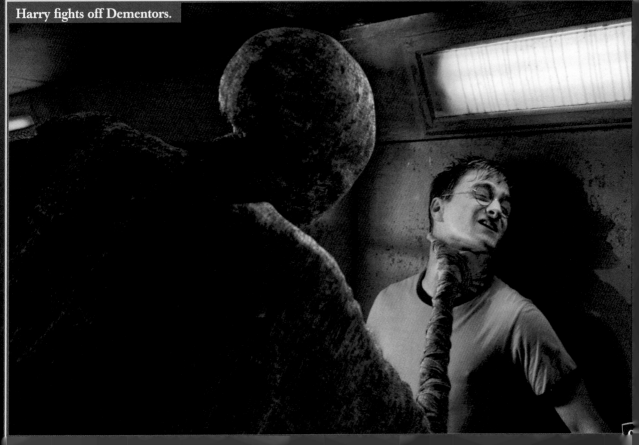

Harry fights off Dementors.

Professor Dumbledore duels with Voldemort.

Lord Voldemort at the Ministry of Magic

Professor Dumbledore battles a serpent conjured by Lord Voldemort.

The Ministry of Magic

The Wizengamot

Cornelius Fudge, former Minister for Magic

Amelia Bones, Head of the Department
of Magical Law Enforcement

Dolores Umbridge,
Senior Undersecretary to the Minister for Magic

Arthur Weasley, Head of the Office for the
Detection and Confiscation of
Counterfeit Defensive Spells and Protective Objects

MAGICAL CREATURES

Fawkes™ the phoenix

Werewolf

Basilisk

Hungarian Horntail dragon

Boggart – in the form of Professor Snape
(Neville's greatest fear)

Boggart – in the form of a giant spider (Ron's greatest fear)

Dementor

Thestral

Sirius Black in Animagus form

Cornish pixie

Mermaid

Centaur

Dobby™ the house-elf

Buckbeak™ the Hippogriff

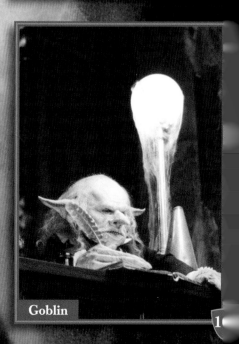

Goblin

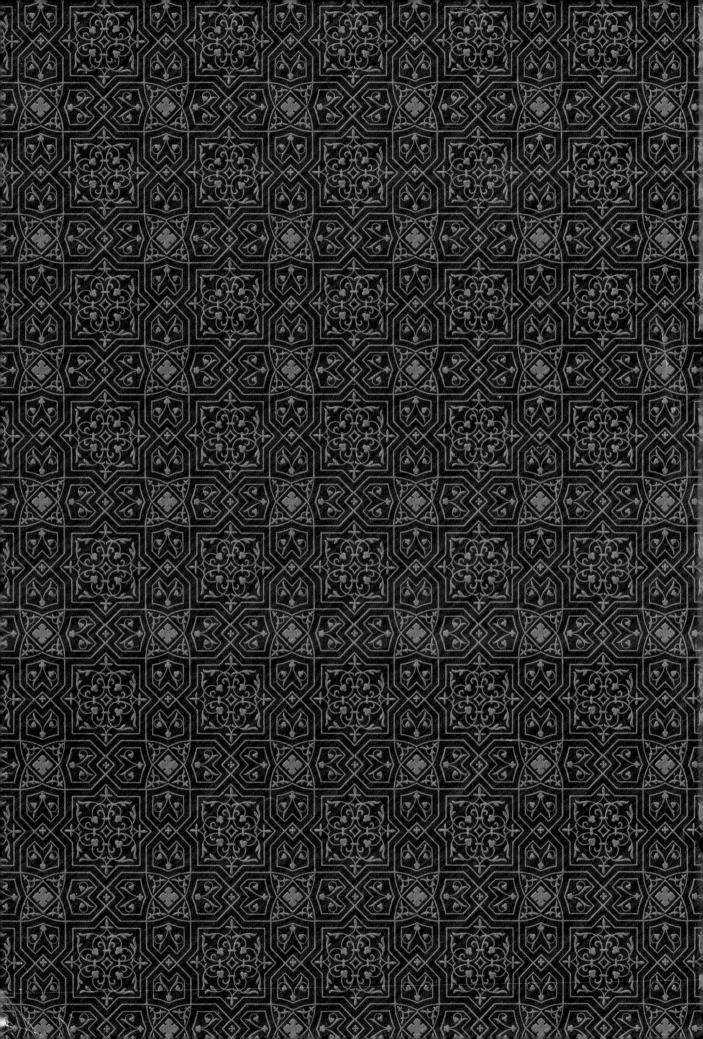